PROSTATE CANCER

Current and Emerging Trends in Detection and Treatment

MARK STOKES, MD, FACP

The Rosen Publishing Group, Inc., New York

To Joanne Gottridge, MD

Published in 2006 by The Rosen Publishing Group, Inc.
29 East 21st Street, New York, NY 10010

First Edition

Library of Congress Cataloging-in-Publication Data

Stokes, Mark.
Prostate cancer: current and emerging trends in detection and treatment / by Mark Stokes.—1st ed.
    p. cm.—(Cancer and modern science)
ISBN 1-4042-0391-5 (library binding)
1. Prostate—Cancer—Juvenile literature.
I. Title. II. Series.
RC280.P7S763 2006
616.99'463—dc22

2005003628

Manufactured in Malaysia

On the cover: Two prostate cancer cells in the final stage of cell division.

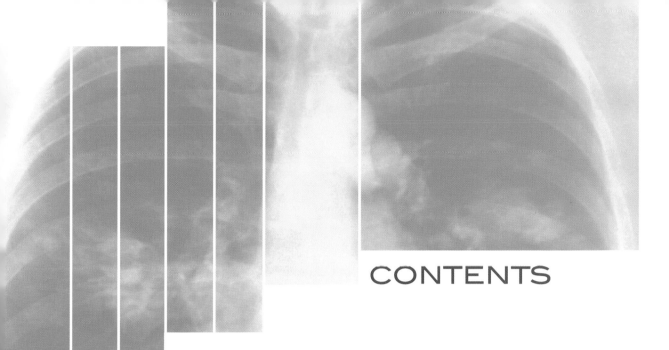

CONTENTS

INTRODUCTION

In recent years, New York Yankees manager Joe Torre, Senators John Kerry and Bob Dole, former secretary of state Colin Powell, former New York City mayor Rudolph Giuliani, and *James Bond* actor Sean Connery have all been diagnosed with prostate cancer. Each year, nearly 200,000 men are diagnosed with the disease. The most common form of cancer in men, prostate cancer is responsible for up to 41,000 deaths per year. It is second only to lung cancer as a cause of cancer-related deaths among men.

It has been estimated that by age fifty, nearly one-third of men will have evidence of prostate cancer. The proportion rises to two-thirds by age seventy. Despite these frightening statistics, it has been found that many more men have prostate cancer than are actually diagnosed with it, and that only a small proportion of those afflicted with the disease will actually die from it. These findings tell us that the disease is one of broad spectrum. In other words, prostate cancer exists in different forms and behaves in different ways. Because of this, the diagnosis and treatment

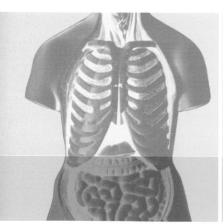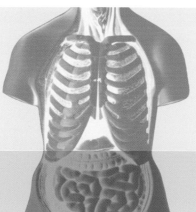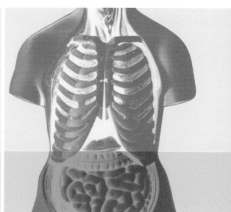

Former senator and presidential candidate Bob Dole emphasizes the importance of screening as he points to a poster of a postal stamp promoting prostate cancer awareness during the National Men's Health and Fitness Conference in Philadelphia, Pennsylvania on June 3, 1999. He was diagnosed with the disease in 1990.

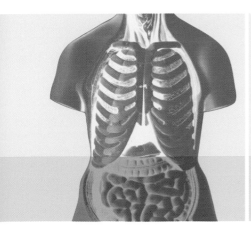
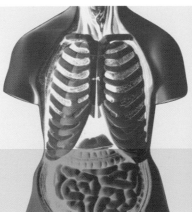
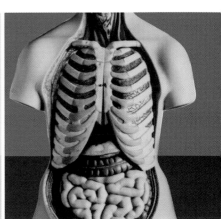

of prostate cancer is one of the biggest controversies in medicine today. It is far from clear who should be tested for the cancer, and if diagnosed, who should be treated.

Nevertheless, medical researchers continue to explore new ways to prevent, diagnose, and treat the disease.

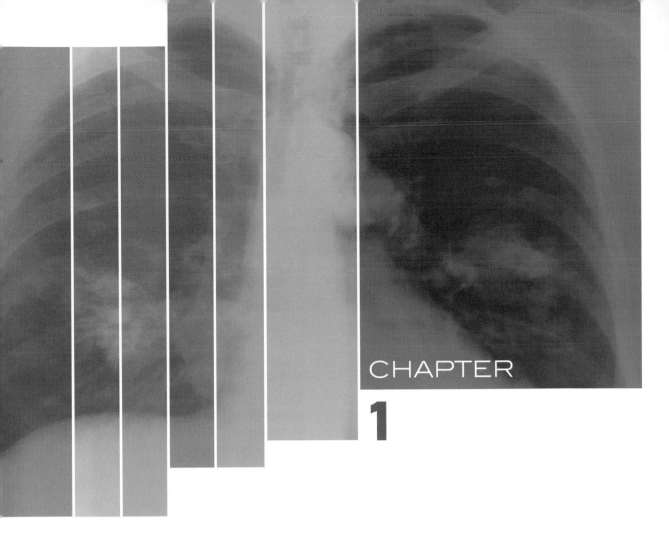

THE PROSTATE: ANATOMY, PHYSIOLOGY, AND PATHOLOGY

Prostate cancer is a male disorder. The reason is simple—only men have prostate glands. In order to understand the dangers of prostate cancer, it is important to study the anatomy (structure), physiology (function), and pathology (disease process) of the prostate.

ANATOMY AND PHYSIOLOGY OF THE PROSTATE

The prostate is a gland that is found deep in the pelvis. Roughly the size of a walnut, it surrounds the neck of the urinary bladder,

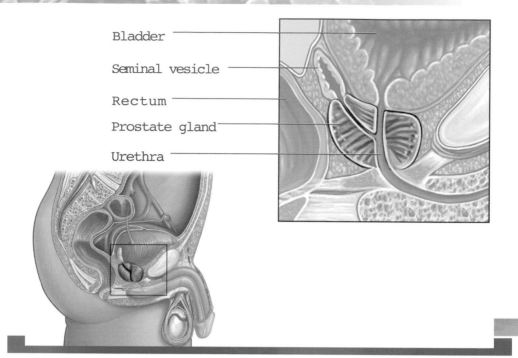

Bladder

Seminal vesicle

Rectum

Prostate gland

Urethra

The prostate gland is a part of the male reproductive system. As illustrated in this diagram, it is located in front of the rectum, where it surrounds the first part of the urethra. Its main function is to produce some of the seminal fluids, which protects and nourishes sperm cells in semen. Also, muscle fibers within the prostate squeeze the urethra slightly, which helps control the flow of urine.

where the urethra, the tube that carries urine, passes through it on its way to the penis. The prostate gland also receives tubes from the testicles, where sperm is produced, and from the seminal vesicles, where, together with the prostate gland itself, the fluid that forms semen is produced. It is the semen that carries sperm during ejaculation.

The prostate gland is composed of glandular cells, which produce the seminal fluid, and muscle cells, which contract during ejaculation to propel the semen forward. On both sides of the prostate gland lie nerves important in sexual function, both erection and ejaculation.

PATHOLOGY

PATHOLOGY

Many diseases can afflict the prostate gland. These include infection, inflammation, and even the development of stones, the way it occurs in the kidney or gallbladder. The most common condition, however, is something called benign prostatic hypertrophy (BPH), which, as will be seen, often imitates prostate cancer and commonly confuses the process of diagnosing the disease.

As males enter adulthood, almost all organs stop growing. Once injured, some, like the heart, are damaged forever. Others, like the skin, can repair themselves, constantly generating new cells. No organ, however, increases in size as men get older, except the prostate gland. Small at birth, and remaining so throughout childhood, the prostate gradually increases in size under the stimulus of testosterone during adolescence. At birth, the prostate is about the size of a pea, less than a tenth of an ounce. During early adolescence, the prostate grows to roughly a third of an ounce. By young adulthood, it increases to a bit more than half an once. By the time a man reaches seventy years of age, the prostate can grow to more than two ounces, the size of a walnut, or even larger.

Because the urethra passes through the prostate as it leaves the bladder, any problem affecting the prostate will interfere with urination in some manner. The most common abnormality involves an impediment to the flow of urine. As the enlarging prostate constricts the urethra, men can experience several symptoms. Hesitancy is the momentary pause between the onset of the urination action and the time when the urine starts to flow out. Urgency is the situation where a man has an uncontrollable desire to urinate. A diminished force of the urine stream also occurs.

As mentioned earlier, the prostate, being a gland, produces different proteins and fluids that are important in semen production and ejaculation.

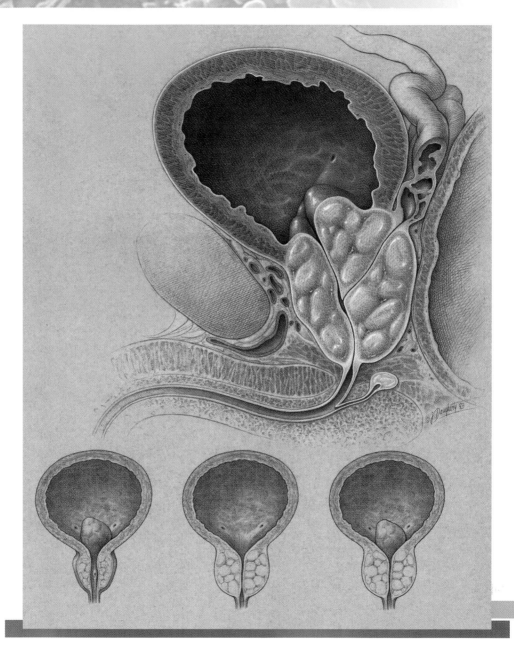

It is common for the gland to become enlarged as a man grows older. This sometimes causes it to constrict the urethra, thereby restricting the flow of urine. This medical illustration shows the normal anatomy of the prostate (top) and three types of prostate enlargement (bottom).

One such protein is called the prostate-specific antigen, or PSA. The amount of PSA produced is directly related to the size of the prostate; that is, the larger the prostate, the more PSA produced. This fact is important in diagnosing prostate cancer.

HOW PROSTATE CANCER DEVELOPS

All cancers, including prostate cancer, develop from damage to DNA (deoxyribonucleic acid). DNA is in every cell of all living things. It is the chemical that carries genetic information and directs nearly all the activities of every cell. As such, it controls everything about the way a person looks. DNA also governs the reproduction of cells in the human body (as well as in all living things). Cells reproduce by growing and dividing. This process is called replication.

Following instructions from the DNA, cell replication generally occurs at a predetermined rate and for a predetermined period. It is influenced by the needs and circumstances of the body. Sometimes a mutation, or structural change, in the DNA of a single cell occurs. When this happens, the cell may acquire the capacity to divide unchecked, at rates faster than "normal" cells, for periods well beyond the normal spans, and regardless of the needs of the body. The result of this excessive cell division is the growth of a tumor, or an abnormal lump of tissue.

Tumors have no useful bodily function. There are two types of tumors: benign and malignant. Benign tumors are typically harmless. Malignant tumors are usually life-threatening, because they can spread to other parts of the body, where they invade and overwhelm other cells. A malignant tumor is a cancer. Prostate cancer is a malignant tumor that originates in the prostate. Although the prostate has several types of cells, more than 99 percent of prostate cancers develop from the glandular cells, according to the American Cancer Society. Cancers that begin in glandular cells are called adenocarcinoma (from the Greek words *aden* for "gland" and *karkinoma* for "cancer").

Because the other forms of prostate cancer are so rare, a person who has been diagnosed with the disease almost certainly has a prostate adenocarcinoma.

RISK FACTORS FOR PROSTATE CANCER

The exact cause of prostate cancer is not known, although many doctors believe it begins with a condition called prostatic intraepithelial neoplasia (PIN). PIN is characterized by changes in the microscopic appearance—for example, size and shape—of prostate gland cells. These changes are classified as either low or high grade, based on the degree of change. Existing research shows that low-grade PIN has no real significance. On the other hand, men who have been diagnosed with a high-grade PIN have a 30 to 50 percent chance of also having prostate cancer. PIN is very common. It begins to appear in men as early as age twenty. Close to half of all men develop the condition by their fiftieth birthday.

Although the exact cause of prostate cancer is unknown, medical researchers have identified a number of risk factors for prostate cancer. These include age, race, nationality, family history, diet, physical inactivity, and obesity.

As discussed earlier, the prostate gland is one of the few organs in the body that can grow slowly but continuously into adulthood. The longer the cells continue to divide, the greater the chance there is to develop one of those mutations that lead to the excessive replication of a cell. As such, age is the single most important risk factor for the development of prostate cancer. Therefore, an eighty-year-old man has a greater chance of developing prostate cancer than a fifty-year-old man, simply because more divisions of cells have occurred, thereby increasing the likelihood of a mutation. According to the American Cancer Society, the chance of developing prostate cancer increases rapidly after age fifty. More than 70 percent of all prostate cancer diagnoses are for men sixty-five years and older.

THE INCIDENCE OF PROSTATE CANCER

Roughly 16 percent (or 1 in 6) of the male population of the United States will be diagnosed with prostate cancer at some point in their lives. Approximately 3 percent (or 1 in 33) will die of the disease. As the following statistics from the Centers for Disease Control and Prevention show, the risk of getting prostate cancer increases with age.

AGE	RISK
45	1 in 2,500
50	1 in 476
55	1 in 120
60	1 in 43
65	1 in 21
70	1 in 9

sumption of red meat, particularly charbroiled meats, is directly correlated to the incidence of prostate cancer. It is believed that chemicals called free radicals, found in high abundance in charbroiled meats, cause DNA mutations resulting in the out-of-control replication of cells. Diets rich in vegetables, especially vegetables with high concentrations of a protein called lycopene, are associated with lower incidences of prostate cancer. They act as "free radical scavengers," reducing these mutation-causing molecules. Men in Asia have a low risk of developing prostate cancer. When they immigrate to westernized countries, such as the United States, their risk substantially increases. Although it is not yet entirely clear why this is so, the difference in such environmental factors as diet has been implicated. Men from areas of the world where the diet

People who eat a lot of grilled red meat are more likely to develop prostate cancer than those who don't. High meat consumption has been implicated in a number of other cancers. Nevertheless, meat is an excellent source of protein. While researchers do not advocate eliminating it from one's diet, they suggest that people eat meat in moderate amounts.

entirely clear why this is so, the difference in such environmental factors as diet has been implicated. Men from areas of the world where the diet is primarily vegetarian, such as Asia, are often less exposed to the free radicals found in cooked meats. Upon relocation to westernized countries, their diets often change to reflect their new locale. Their intake of cooked meats increases, thereby exposing them to free radicals.

Furthermore, poor eating habits combined with lack of physical exercise can lead to obesity, an excessive accumulation of body fat which makes one very overweight. Recent studies show that there is a strong link between obesity and the incidence of prostate cancer. They also suggest that when obesity develops at a young age, the chance of developing a more aggressive form of prostate cancer increases.

Genetics also has much to do with the risk of prostate cancer. Among the proteins that are made under the direction of DNA are enzymes that actually repair mutations. These enzymes themselves may be malformed, causing them to lose the ability to correct damaged DNA. It is known that prostate cancer is more prevalent in African Americans and in families in which other males have had the disease. According to the American Cancer Society, African American men are 60 percent more likely to develop prostate cancer and twice as likely to die from the disease than white men. For all men, having a brother or father with prostate cancer doubles a man's risk of developing the disease. It is quite possible that mutations to the DNA-repairing genes are passed from generation to generation, with persistent risk. Forty-two percent of cases of prostate cancer are attributed to genetics.

Finally, chronic or recurrent inflammation has been associated with prostate cancer. Any type of inflammation, as might be seen in some types of sexually transmitted diseases, damages the cells of the prostate. As the cells repair themselves, they do so with an increased likelihood of triggering a mutation that can lead to cancer.

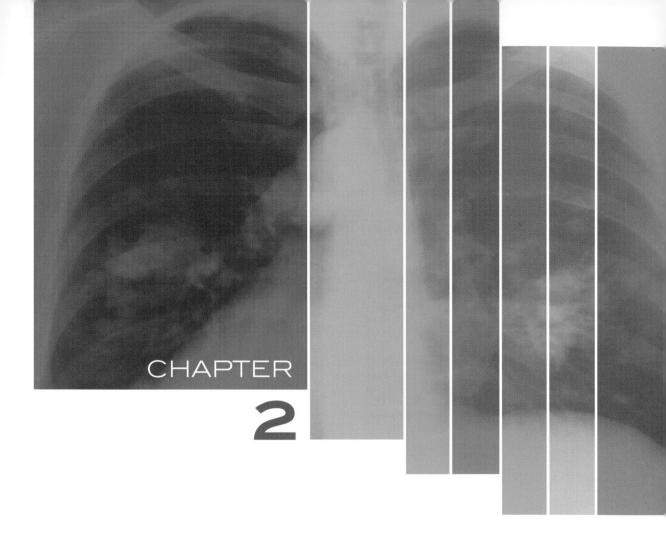

SCREENING AND DIAGNOSING PROSTATE CANCER

As is true for all types of cancers, the sooner prostate cancer is detected, the greater the options available to the patient and his physician for treating the disease and the greater the chances of achieving a cure. Accordingly, the American Cancer Society recommends that men be screened annually for prostate cancer once they become fifty years old. For men who are considered at high risk (such as African Americans and those with a family history), the organization recommends that they begin screening at age forty. For reasons that will soon become clear, there is

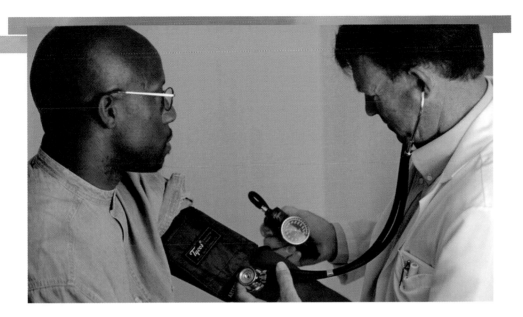

Medical research shows that African American men develop prostate cancer at a higher rate than do men of every other ethnic group in the United States. For this reason, the medical community recommends that they begin screening by age forty, ten years sooner than the recommendation for other men of average risk.

considerable debate within the medical community over the value of annual screening.

The purpose of any cancer screening test is to find a malignancy before the patient begins to show symptoms, before the cancer has spread, and to treat it in hopes of reducing the mortality (death) rate from it. As screening for other types of cancers have been shown to make a difference—for example, a mammography for breast cancer; a pap smear for cervical cancer; and a colonoscopy for colon cancer—it was hoped that prostate cancer screening would increase life expectancy for men with the disease. Unfortunately, the evidence to date is inconclusive, and existing data demonstrate that prostate cancer screening has been found wanting.

This medical illustration shows a physician conducting a digital rectal exam on the prostate gland. This screening test gives the doctor an indication of the size of the prostate gland and whether there are any irregular or abnormally firm areas. By itself, the DRE does not determine whether the patient has prostate cancer. It can only suggest the need for more tests.

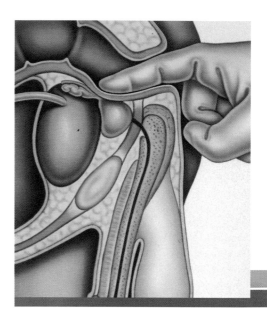

DIGITAL RECTAL EXAM (DRE)

Until 1987, the only way that a doctor could detect for the presence of prostate cancer was through a digital rectal exam, or DRE. To perform this screening method, the physician inserts his or her gloved finger into a patient's rectum, and feels along its anterior, or front, wall. As explained earlier, the prostate gland sits directly in front of the rectum. During the examination, the doctor tries to assess if there is any asymmetry (that is, any lack of balance in size and shape), nodularity (bumpiness, from the presence of tumor nodules) or induration (firmness) in the gland. Any of these conditions might be evidence of a cancer. The problem with this test is that only the back one-third of the gland is within reach. As a result, there is no way of determining if the front two-thirds is abnormal. In fact, even if something can be felt on examination, there is a 50 percent chance that a cancer, if present, has already spread beyond the gland.

PROSTATE-SPECIFIC ANTIGEN (PSA) TEST

Discovered in 1979 and first used clinically in 1987, the prostate-specific antigen (PSA) test changed the way physicians were able to diagnose prostate cancer. Once the test became available, the annual incidence of prostate cancer increased dramatically   more prostate cancers were being found. Though some physicians and medical researchers thought this was the "magic answer" in finding and treating prostate cancer, the use of the PSA test did not translate into a survival benefit. Despite more prostate cancers being found and treated earlier, the annual mortality rate did not substantially change. What was going on?

One answer lay in what is termed "lead-time bias." Suppose two men, each age fifty, developed prostate cancer on the same day. The first man sees his doctor for an examination and a PSA test, and the prostate cancer is found. He undergoes treatment, does well for a time, but dies from the cancer at age sixty-five. It is said he survived fifteen years with his cancer. The second man does not see a doctor until he is age sixty, when he begins to have symptoms of prostate disease. At that point, he is diagnosed with and treated for prostate cancer, but he, too, dies from the cancer at age sixty-five. It is said that he survived only five years with his cancer, and that the first man lived three times as long because of prostate cancer screening. But if you look more closely at the numbers, both men lived exactly the same amount of time with the cancer; the only difference is that the first man knew about the cancer three times as long.

Another reason why the use of PSA testing has not substantially changed the mortality rate from prostate cancer has to do with the wide spectrum of behavior that the tumors can exhibit. A prostate cancer can be very aggressive, with rapid growth and metastasis (spread); or it can by very indolent, growing slowly and remaining confined to the gland, in effect

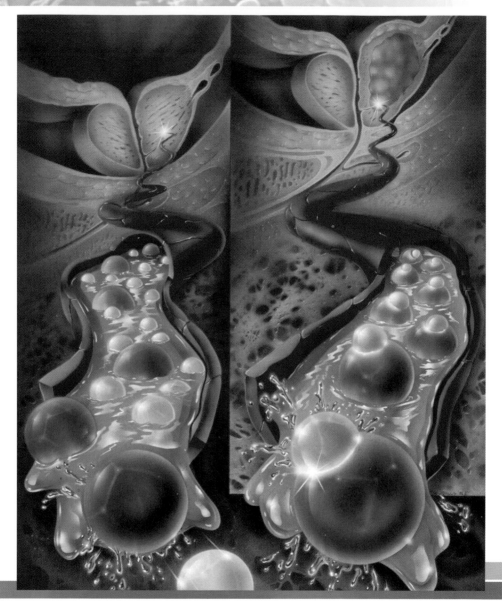

This illustration shows the connection between prostate cancer and the level of PSA. On the left is a healthy prostate; on the right is a cancerous one. In both panels, yellow spheres represent the dye used to test for PSA, and blue spheres represent prostate proteins. On the right, the dye molecules attach themselves to proteins that cancer has changed into PSA, making them detectable in a blood test. Note that the test is conducted on a blood sample, and not in the body.

never affecting the health of the man; or it can be somewhere between these two extremes. A PSA level does not allow physicians to distinguish among these scenarios. Twenty percent of aggressive tumors have levels well within what is considered normal. Levels well above the normal range are associated with cancer only 40 to 60 percent of the time.

Another reason that PSA readings can be problematic has to do with false positives, a test result indicating a problem where one does not exist. Recent ejaculation, prostate inflammation, or benign prostatic hypertrophy can raise PSA levels in the absence of cancer. It has been estimated that as many as 60 percent of positive readings fall into this category.

All this leads to a sort of Pandora's box of further problems: having a negative test can lead to a false sense of security despite the presence of cancer, or a positive test can lead a person to doing further testing and treatments for a disease that might not exist or, if it does, might never affect his life.

It is because the DRE and the PSA tests, both separately and together, cannot give a definitive result as to the presence of prostate cancer that many major scientific and medical organizations, including the Centers for Disease Control and Prevention and the National Cancer Institute, do not advocate annual screening at this time. They recognize that inconclusive results can lead to confusion and anxiety.

Nevertheless, the existing screening measures for prostate cancer can be performed easily and quickly in a physician's office. A positive result is not equal to a diagnosis for cancer, but it is an indication that further testing for cancer may be required.

PROSTATE CANCER SYMPTOMS

The symptoms of prostate cancer, much like cancer itself, can vary greatly. Very often, a man may have no symptoms, and would not know he had a cancer unless his physician specifically went looking for it. Many of the symptoms, like that of benign prostatic hypertrophy (BPH), have

OBESITY AND PSA RESULTS

As we have already learned, obesity is one of the risk factors for the development of prostate cancer. But as researchers from the University of Texas Health Science Center in San Antonio, Texas, reported in January 2005, obesity may affect the accuracy of the PSA screening test, as obesity is inversely related to PSA level (that is, the greater the weight, the lower the PSA level). As such, an obese man might actually have prostate cancer despite having a "normal" PSA level. The researchers say that their findings may help explain why obese men are more likely to be diagnosed when their cancer is more advanced and why they are more likely to die from the disease. The findings are particularly significant, considering that more than 27 percent of American men are obese.

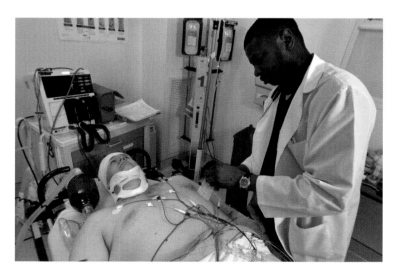

Obesity results from consuming far more calories than the body uses, usually reflecting a combination of poor nutritional habits and an inactive lifestyle. In addition to its role in the development and detection of prostate cancer, obesity also influences other life-threatening disorders.

to do with the constriction the prostate places on the bladder outlet. These include urgency to urinate, frequency of urination, and hesitancy. Prostate cancers sometimes bleed, and blood can at times be seen in the urine, a symptom known as hematuria. Because the nerves guiding sexual function are very close to the gland, erection problems can sometimes be the presenting (initial) feature of prostate cancer. Sometimes the first manifestation of prostate cancer will be evidence that it has metastasized, or spread, beyond the gland. The spinal bones are the most common sites of this spread.

DIAGNOSING PROSTATE CANCER

Once the decision has been made that a man has symptoms, positive indications of cancer from a digital rectal exam, or a PSA value suspicious for prostate cancer, the patient's primary care physician would most likely refer him to a urologist, a doctor who specializes in prostate-related problems. The urologist would likely perform a biopsy of the prostate to prove or disprove the existence of cancer. This is accomplished with the assistance of an ultrasound probe. This probe is inserted into the rectum, which is just behind the prostate gland. Ultrasound gives something like a radar picture of the gland, and may reveal irregular areas to target for biopsy.

During the ultrasound-guided biopsy, a needle is passed through the rectum into the gland, removing small bits of tissue. This is usually done six to eight times to obtain random samples in all areas of the gland. This tissue is then sent to a lab, where a pathologist, a doctor who identifies diseases by studying cells and tissues under a microscope, will examine it to determine if cancer is indeed present.

If the pathologist detects cancer, he or she will assign it a grade. Most pathologists grade prostate cancer using the Gleason system, which has five grades from 1 to 5 that indicate the degree to which the cancerous tissue looks like normal prostate tissue. A grade 1 tumor closely resembles

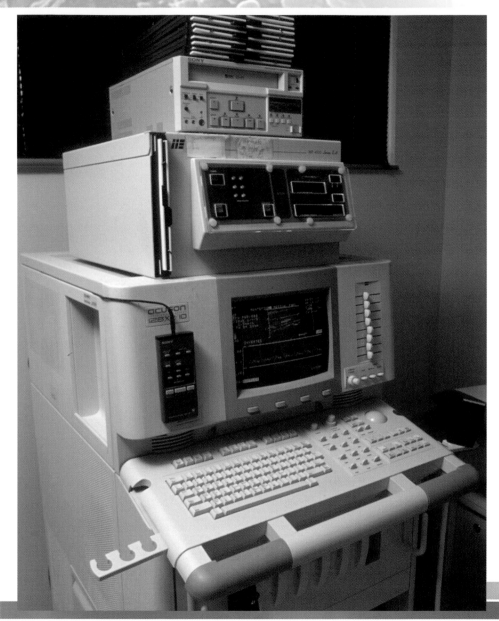

An ultrasound machine is basically a specialized computer that uses sound waves to examine and treat hard-to-reach areas of the body. Originally developed during World War I to detect submerged objects, the technology now has many medical applications, including determining the sex of a fetus, detecting heart damage, and relieving pain in the joints.

the normal tissue. A grade 5 tumor shows marked differences. It is common for different parts of the cancer to have different grades. Therefore, the pathologist grades the two areas that make up most of the cancer, then adds the two grades to come up with a Gleason score between 2 and 10. The Gleason score signals whether the cancer will grow and spread rapidly.

However, the pathologist's determination may not be 100 percent accurate. Even in the instance where the patient has six negative biopsies, there is still a 10 percent chance that he has prostate cancer. If you think of the prostate gland as a golf ball, and a cancer as a grain of rice within that golf ball, it is easy to see how randomly passing a needle through the ball can easily miss the grain of rice.

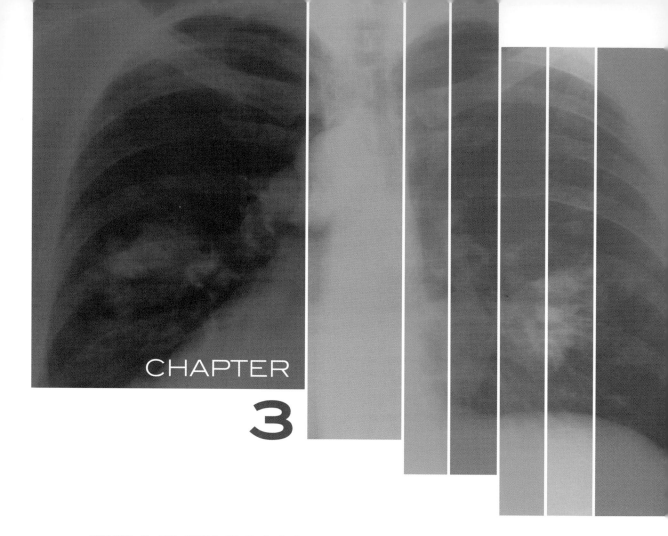

CHAPTER

3

TRADITIONAL AND NEW TREATMENTS

Once diagnosed with prostate cancer, the man must decide with his physician whether and how to treat the disease. The type of treatment will depend on factors related to the cancer, such as the extent of the disease, and factors related to the patient, such as age and the presence of other medical conditions. After diagnosis, most patients will undergo a CAT (computerized axial tomography) scan of the pelvis and a nuclear bone scan. The CAT scan can visualize the areas surrounding the prostate gland, including local lymph nodes. A CAT scan is a three-dimensional X-ray of an area

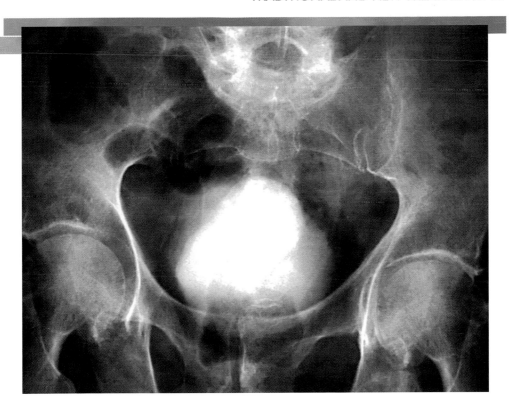

This colored X-ray of a male pelvis shows an enlarged prostate gland as two dark indentations at the bottom of the bladder (white, lower center). Enlargement of the prostate, which may be caused by prostate cancer, can obstruct the passing of urine through the urethra, which may in turn damage the kidneys.

of the body, constructed with a sophisticated computer. The X-rays allow a radiologist to "see" inside the body. Lymph nodes, collections of immune tissue present to fight infection and inflammation, appear on the scan as grayish circles. By comparing the size of the lymph nodes to what would be considered normal, the radiologist is able to predict whether or not they contain cancerous cells. The bone scan looks for evidence of the spread of cancer to the spinal bones. Should either test reveal that the cancer has spread beyond the confines of the gland itself, treatment

STAGING PROSTATE CANCER

The process of determining how far cancer has metastasized, or spread, is called staging. Doctors use a combination of the patient's DRE results, PSA level, Gleason score, and, if needed, the results from CAT and/or bone scans to stage the disease.

Progression of Prostate Cancer

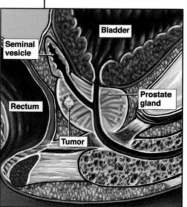

Early Stage Prostate Cancer

- Bladder
- Seminal vesicle
- Rectum
- Prostate gland
- Tumor

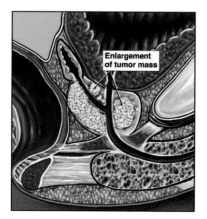

Subsequent Condition

- Enlargement of tumor mass

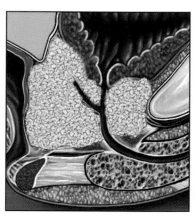

Eventual Condition

Sagittal views

This medical illustration demonstrates how prostate cancer spreads if left untreated. However, in many instances, the progression of prostate cancer may occur so slowly that it never affects a man's overall health. Nevertheless, the treatment options are greater during the earlier stages of the disease than for cancer that has spread beyond the prostate.

The most widely used staging system in the United States is the American Joint Committee on Cancer's TNM system. The staging system describes the size and extent of the primary tumor (the T element); whether the cancer has spread to nearby lymph nodes (the N element); and the metastasis (the M element) to distant lymph nodes, bones, and other organs. The TNM system has four stages, which are described as follows:

Stage 1: The cancer is limited to the prostate gland, has a low Gleason score, and less than 5 percent of the tissue is cancerous.

Stage 2: The cancer is limited to the prostate gland, but has a Gleason score above 4, was discovered by a high PSA level, can be detected by a DRE, or can be seen during a transrectal ultrasound.

Stage 3: The cancer has begun to spread outside the prostate to the seminal vesicles, but has not yet affected the lymph nodes or any other part of the body.

Stage 4: The cancer has spread to tissues next to the prostate, lymph nodes, and to other tissues and organs far away from the prostate.

The stage of cancer influences the treatment options available to the patient and his physician and the patient's chances of recovery and survival.

directed at the gland itself will be ineffective, and a more systemic, or "whole body" approach must be taken.

DOING NOTHING AND WATCHFUL WAITING

One treatment option is to do nothing at all. This is an appropriate strategy for men who are elderly or have severe illnesses, such as end-stage heart disease. In these instances, a man has an equal or greater chance of dying from something else, such as the heart disease, as he does of dying from the prostate cancer. He may be so ill that he may not survive the treatment for the cancer. Clearly, in such a situation, treating the prostate cancer does more harm than good.

But what about younger, healthy men? Is it ever appropriate to do nothing? In some instances it is. Sometimes the pathologist, who views the biopsy specimens, can make a determination as to the aggressiveness of the tumor by examining the features of the cancer cells. Tumor cells that are very similar to normal cells are termed "well-differentiated" and they may mimic the behavior of normal prostate cells. The patient, knowing that this type of cancer may grow very slowly, might opt for a strategy known as watchful waiting. This strategy means not treating the tumor unless it starts to cause health problems. Here he is, in a sense, gambling that he will "outlive" the cancer. As many prostate cancers are at this indolent, or slow, end of the spectrum, the gamble might not be so great.

SURGICAL PROCEDURES

Should the patient and his physician decide to treat the prostate cancer, the next decision is whether to treat it surgically or nonsurgically. The surgical treatment involves removing the prostate gland. This type of surgery is known as a prostatectomy. Depending upon the skill and preference of the surgeon, and sometimes technical factors related to

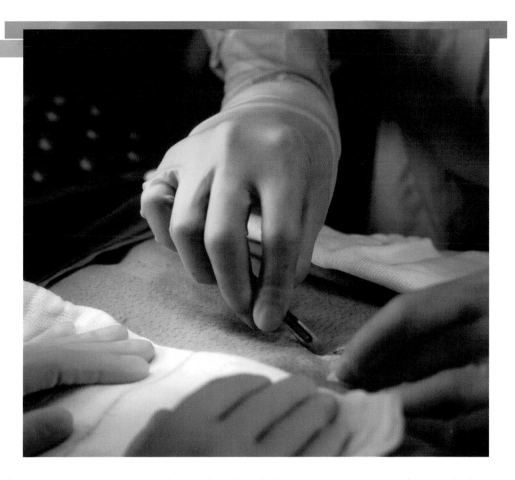

A surgeon prepares to make an incision during a prostatectomy, the surgical removal of the prostate gland. Prostatectomy is a major operation that requires hospitalization and can produce side effects related to urinary and sexual function.

the patient or the tumor itself, the prostatectomy can be performed in one of several ways, related to where the surgical incision gets made.

The oldest type of procedure, called the radical perineal prostatectomy, was first done in 1905. In this procedure, an incision is made in

This medical illustration shows the removal of a prostate gland. This treatment option is usually performed on patients whose cancers are at an early stage, and who are therefore more likely to be cured. However, it is sometimes done to relieve symptoms of more advanced prostate cancers.

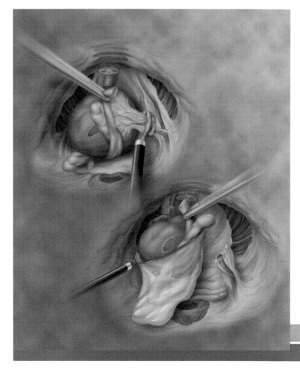

the perineal region, the area behind the scrotum and in front of the rectum. The prostate is then dissected away from the surrounding tissue, and removed. In 1947, the first retropubic prostatectomy was performed. Here, the incision is made in the lower abdominal wall, about halfway between the navel and the penis. As in the radical perineal prostatectomy, the prostate is dissected and removed.

In recent years, laparoscopic prostatectomy has revolutionized the surgical approach to treating prostate cancer. Recovery from either the perineal or retropubic surgeries was long and arduous, quite painful, and required a prolonged hospital stay. Because of the extent of the surgery, infection was not uncommon, and because of the need for bed rest, a complication such as blood clots in the leg was a risk.

The laparoscopic approach substantially reduced these postoperative problems. In laparoscopic surgery, several small incisions—each less than an inch (2.5 centimeters)—are made in the abdominal wall, usually in the navel and to the sides. Next, carbon dioxide is pumped into the abdominal cavity, distending (expanding) it. Then, an instrument with a camera on the end is introduced into the cavity through one of the small incisions. Video from inside the abdomen is projected onto a TV screen. It is almost like seeing the inside of a basketball without cutting it open. Other surgical instruments, which are able to dissect, cut, and suture (sew up), are put through the other incisions, and the surgeon operates them while watching where they are inside the abdomen on the video screen. In this way, the surgeon locates the prostate gland, cuts it out, and removes it through one of the incisions. It is much like playing a video game, and many of the same skills are required. In fact, during their training periods, surgeons practice on simulators that are like video games. Once the surgery is complete, the instruments are removed, and the incisions are closed (sometimes with nothing more than a Band-Aid!). The bloodstream absorbs the carbon dioxide.

Because the extent of the laparoscopic surgery is much less than the traditional surgeries, the recovery period is much easier and shorter. Patients are usually up and about within a day, and they go home much sooner than they would have with the other procedures. Moreover, because the surgical incisions are so tiny, the chances of infection are fewer.

The real problem with any of the surgical procedures lies in the probable damage to the surrounding structures. Remember that the urethra, the tube leading from the urinary bladder, passes through the prostate, and the nerves controlling sexual function lie on both sides of it. Depending on the skill of the surgeon, the size of the tumor, and many other factors, those structures are sometimes easily damaged. This can result in incontinence, impotence, or the inability to achieve an orgasm. These effects may be temporary, but they may also be permanent. Such problems can be devastating to a man, especially to someone who wants to have children. Urinary incontinence, the inability to control urination,

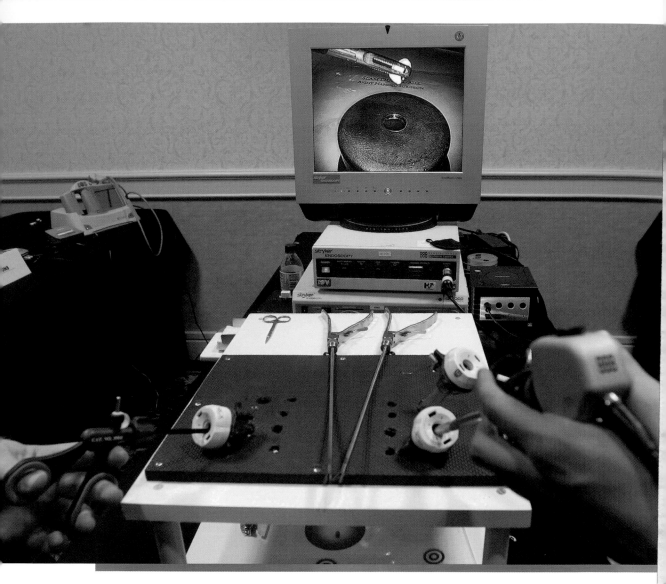

Laparoscopic surgeons and medical students practice on simulators, such as the one pictured here during a demonstration at the 2004 Video Game Entertainment Industry Technology and Medicine Conference in Marina Del Ray, California. Laparoscopic surgery is somewhat similar to playing video games in that the surgeon must rely on good hand-eye coordination and the skillful use of controllers and a small screen. Research shows that surgeons who play video games moved faster and made fewer mistakes during laparoscopic surgery than those who do not.

can be socially embarrassing. Still, if the prostate cancer has not spread at the time of surgery, and if the tumor is removed in its entirety, a man may be willing to take these risks, as successful surgery offers a tremendous chance of curing the disease.

While surgery has the best chance of curing disease, it has been estimated that up to 14 percent of prostatectomies are done for clinically insignificant tumors—that is, those tumors that, had they been left alone, would not have caused problems for the patient. Because surgery has a number of side effects, the patient might opt for a different type of therapy designed to destroy the tumor, but with less risk of troubling complications. These therapies usually involve radiation of some type.

CHEMOTHERAPY AND RADIATION THERAPY

Earlier it was discussed how DNA governs the growth of cells, and how it is believed that mutations in the DNA structure might lead to changes in a cell's function. These changes can cause the cell to grow unchecked as a cancer. However, the integrity of the DNA must be preserved to some degree, otherwise critical functions of the cell would cease, and the cell would die. The ability to induce lethal mutations in DNA structure lies at the foundation of nonsurgical cancer treatment. By changing the structure of DNA, chemotherapy and radiation prevent normal cell reproduction and cause the cell to die off. Chemotherapy, which is the practice of using chemicals in an attempt to treat a disease, is one way to accomplish this. By infusing drugs into the bloodstream that have a predilection for certain types of tumors, many types of cancers can be destroyed. Unfortunately, although many have been tried, no one particular type of chemotherapy has been proven to be efficient against prostate cancer cells. Radiation therapy, however, has been found to be quite effective.

A nurse administers chemotherapy to an elderly man as his sister looks on. Most often, the drug is given intravenously (through a vein), the method pictured here. It may also be given by mouth or by injection, or it can be applied to the skin.

EXTERNAL BEAM RADIATION THERAPY

Radiation can be directed at a cancerous prostate gland in one of several ways. One of the oldest methods is known as external beam radiation therapy. In this procedure, a machine, much like a regular X-ray machine, beams radiation waves through the body into the prostate gland. Low levels are used on a daily basis, for only a few minutes a day, but over several weeks, such that a patient may receive perhaps thirty or forty dosages of radiation. One major disadvantage of this technique, however, is that not only the bad prostate cancer cells are attacked by the radiation. The normal cells that lie around them are attacked, too. Therefore, while those lethal mutations are induced in the cancer cells, they also destroy the good cells.

3D-CRT AND CONFORMAL PROTON BEAM RADIATION THERAPY

In recent years, a number of techniques have been developed to try to limit the amount of radiation that the good cells are exposed to, while maximizing the amount that reaches the prostate. One such type is known as three-dimensional conformal radiation therapy (3D-CRT). With this technique, sophisticated computers construct a three-dimensional model of the patient's prostate tumor. The computers then direct the radiation tubes to fire very small amounts of radiation from 360 degrees around the patient toward the tumor in such a way that the radiation rays all meet in the prostate gland, and only in the prostate gland.

Another method is known as conformal proton beam radiation therapy. In this technique, beams of protons are used instead of conventional radiation rays, but are delivered in the same 3D way. The benefit of this is that the protons pass through normal tissue doing little damage, until they all converge in the prostate tumor.

The advantage of these latter two methods over conventional external beam radiation is that the radiation is concentrated in the prostate. In this way, the amount of radiation to which surrounding tissues are exposed is minimized, and the amount the prostate receives is maximized. The disadvantages of any type of external radiation therapy are that the treatment course can be very long, often forty sessions over eight weeks, and there is usually at least some damage to the surrounding tissues. This damage can be as mild as a

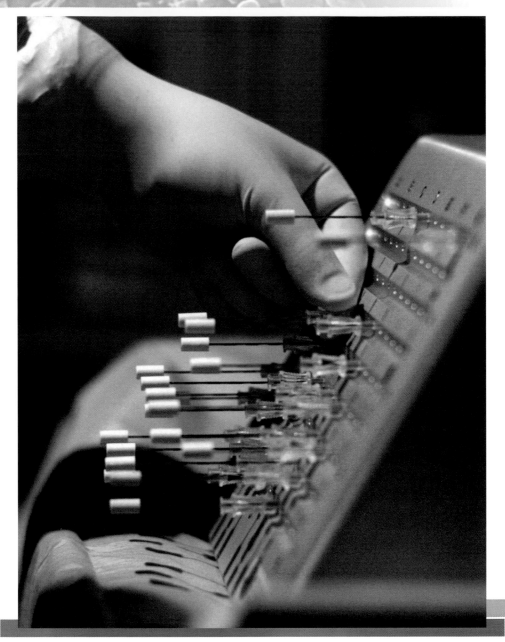

A physician removes needles containing radioactive seeds from a rack to implant into a prostate cancer patient undergoing brachytherapy. The seeds are placed either in tumors or near them. This treatment allows the surgeon to minimize radiation damage to normal tissues.

slight skin burn, similar to a sunburn, or as serious as bowel damage, with bloody diarrhea that might last for years. Another disadvantage of radiation is that it does not provide the surgical opportunity to biopsy surrounding tissues in order to get a better idea of the extent of the disease.

BRACHYTHERAPY, CRYOTHERAPY, AND MICROWAVE THERAPY

Yet another type of radiation therapy is known as brachytherapy. In this type of treatment, tiny pellets of radioactive material—smaller than grains of rice—are surgically implanted into the prostate. This radioactive material can be either palladium or iodine. These pellets, or "seeds," deliver radiation directly to the prostate tumor from within the tumor. When the radiation enters cells, it causes the formation of particles called free radicals, which then damage the DNA. These seeds can be of an element that gives off low-intensity radiation, and they are left in for days to weeks to years, exposing the tumor to the lethal effects over a very long period of time. Or the seeds can be of an element that gives off large amounts of radiation, and left in for only a short period of time, usually less than a day. Some seeds are left in permanently, their duration of effect determined by the type of radioactive material and its half life. When the radioactivity ceases, the effects stop, though the seed—in which the radioactive material is imbedded—remains in the body. Other types are left in only for a few minutes. The duration of this therapy is measured in terms of number of sessions, and is influenced by the size of the tumor. Algorithms (advanced formulas or procedures for solving problems) are used to correlate total radiation dose to the volume of the tumor. The advantage of brachytherapy is that exposure of normal tissue to the deadly radioactive rays is really minimal, so side effects are not so terrible. The main side effect seems to be rectal pain.

This is a metal cryoprobe, used to treat prostate cancer in cryotherapy, and its control panel. The ice ball at the probe's tip demonstrates its cooling power after being placed in water. During cryotherapy, the probe is inserted into the prostate gland (through the skin between the scrotum and the rectum), where it freezes and kills nearby cancer cells.

An exciting new type of therapy for prostate cancer is known as cryotherapy. In this type of treatment, a small probe, perhaps no larger than a wire, is passed through the perineum, that area between the rectum and the scrotum, into the prostate gland. The wire is then "super-cooled," to temperatures far below 0° Fahrenheit (−17.22° Celsius). As this happens, the water inside the cells that are near the probe freezes. Later, as the ice crystals melt, the cells become damaged and burst open, destroying themselves. While this therapy seems promising, not enough study has yet been done on it to see if it is as effective as some of the other types of treatments.

Another very new type of treatment is microwave therapy. In this type of treatment, wires are again inserted through the skin into the prostate. But instead of being cooled, the wires are heated with microwaves to temperatures over 100°F (37.78°C), vaporizing the tumor. Like cryotherapy, this technique has not been studied enough to demonstrate its effectiveness.

CHOOSING AMONG TREATMENT OPTIONS

It may seem difficult to decide which therapy is best for which patient. Certainly, concerns about side effects and other medical problems need to be considered. However, the general rule is that some type of surgical procedure is appropriate for men younger than age seventy, and radiation therapy for men older than seventy, when either group has more than ten years of life expectancy.

What, then, of men with less than ten years of life expectancy, or those men in whom the prostate cancer has spread beyond the confines of the prostate gland itself? Clearly, such aggressive therapies as surgery or radiation make little sense, as the treatments, and their attendant risks and side effects, would not add much to a man's life expectancy, nor would they treat the disease that has spread beyond the prostate. In such instances, the patient and his physician have a number of options.

As mentioned earlier, one option would be to do nothing. Many types of prostate cancers are very slow growing and cause no problems for the patient's health. A very elderly patient, particularly one with many other health problems—such as heart disease, diabetes, etc.—may elect to do nothing, recognizing that his other diseases may end his life well

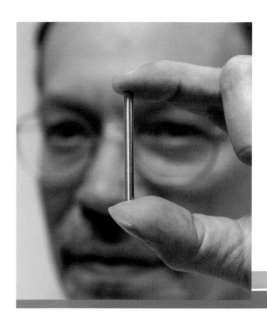

Urologist Dr. Craig Zippe displays a Viadur implant in his office on March 28, 2001. The inch-and-a-half-long (3.8-cm) titanium tube is implanted into the upper arm of a cancer patient and dispenses leuprolide over a period of one year. A form of hormone therapy, the drug relieves prostate cancer symptoms by lowering the patient's testosterone level. However, it does not cure the disease.

before the prostate cancer would. It is thus perfectly reasonable to ignore the cancer, or merely treat whatever symptoms it may cause.

Another possibility is to take advantage of the fact that the prostate gland responds to hormone levels. It was mentioned earlier that the gland starts to grow when males enter puberty, because of the influence of testosterone. It is possible to manipulate the levels of testosterone in a cancer patient's body in order to arrest the growth of a cancer. This can be achieved in one of several ways.

The simplest and most effective is to perform an orchiectomy. This is a surgical procedure in which both testicles are removed. As the testes are the main source of testosterone in men, their removal will cause the level of the hormone to drop to nearly zero, and the stimulus for any prostate cells to grow will be lost. While the thought of such surgery is somewhat psychologically disturbing, the procedure is quite effective and permanent, removing the need for continued treatments, such as those that follow.

It may also be possible to manipulate the testes to stop producing testosterone. The testes produce testosterone under the influence of pituitary hormones known as gonadotropins. The production of gonadotropins can be blocked by a medication known as leuprolide. With no gonadotropins around to influence the testes, the testes make no testosterone, and there is nothing to stimulate the prostate cancer cells. It is also possible to use a medication called flutamide. Flutamide prevents testosterone from binding to cells, and keeps it from influencing growth.

Of course, the absence of testosterone does have some negative side effects. Among these are the loss of interest in sexual activity and the development of gynecomastia, which is the development of breast tissue in a man. Still, these side effects are not as problematic as the side effects of radiation or surgery.

FOLLOW-UP

No matter the type of treatment approach to prostate cancer, the patient's health care team will monitor him to see if the cancer recurs (reappears) or spreads further. The follow-up plan will likely include regular doctor visits, digital rectal exams, and PSA blood tests. It may also include bone scans and other imaging tests. These follow-up visits are crucial to the recovery and general welfare of the patient.

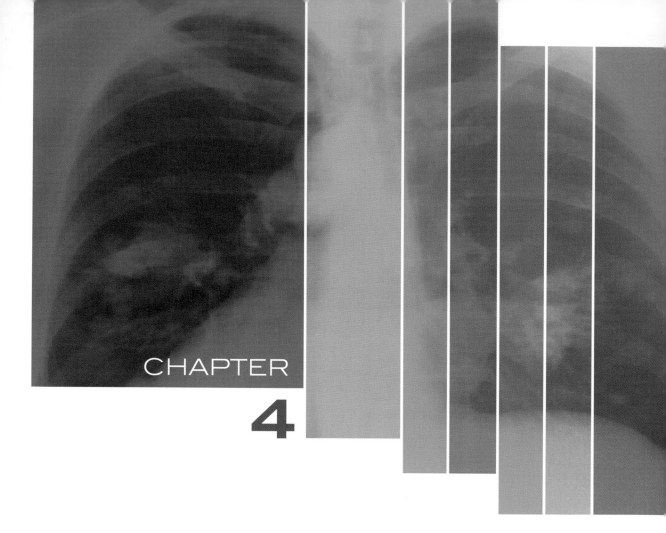

CHAPTER

4

EMERGING TECHNOLOGIES IN PROSTATE CANCER TREATMENT

The future of treatment of prostate cancer is exciting. Scientists are working on three unique therapies, which are or soon will be undergoing clinical trials. (A clinical trial is a scientific study involving human subjects, designed to measure the effectiveness of new medicines and procedures.) Recognizing that the basis of cancer is the alteration of genes that control cell growth, scientists are working on a technique to insert new genes into the prostate cancer cells. These new genes could either restore the normal genes, allowing the cells to regain regulation over their growth, or act as lethal genes, forcing the cells to self-destruct. The manner of inserting the genes into the cells is actually quite interesting. The genes are first incorporated into a type of organism known as an adenovirus. These viruses have been designed specifically to infect prostate cells. The viruses are injected into the bloodstream, where they seek out prostate tissue, attaching to it and inserting the new genes into the DNA. This technology, known as gene therapy, is believed to be quite safe and free of side effects, as the virus is designed to infect only prostate cells, preventing the insertion of the manipulated genes into any other tissue.

The surface of every cell contains unique proteins that identify itself to the body's immune system as being part of the body. It is by this manner that the immune system can distinguish normal cells from such invaders as bacteria and viruses. When cancer cells develop, sometimes these surface proteins become altered. These altered surface proteins can be isolated, purified, and produced in large quantities. They can then be injected into the body and act as a vaccine. The vaccine induces the immune system to recognize the prostate cancer cells as foreign invaders, and so destroys them.

CONCLUSION

Especially since major public figures such as Joe Torre and Rudolph Giuliani have made their prostate cancer diagnoses public, the media have stepped up their coverage of prostate cancer. This increased media attention has raised public awareness about the disease, as well as funding for research. Celebrities with prostate cancer have urged men to get screened, reinforcing the truth that early detection increases a man's chances of beating the disease.

Unfortunately, because we do not know the exact cause or causes of prostate cancer, it is not possible to prevent most cases of the disease at this time. Moreover, many of the risk factors, such as age, race, and genetics cannot be controlled. Nevertheless, there are certain things

African American men sign up for a free prostate cancer screening by a mobile screening unit at an NAACP convention in Philadelphia. The mobile unit was sponsored by the National Prostate Cancer Coalition in an effort to raise awareness among African American men, who are considered a high-risk group for developing the disease.

New York Yankees manager Joe Torre (left) poses with Dr. William Catalona at the 2004 Major League Baseball All Star Game. Catalona, the urologic surgeon who operated on Torre for prostate cancer, is the developer of the PSA test for screening the disease. He is also the medical director for the Urological Research Foundation, which supports research in prostate cancer.

that men can do to reduce the likelihood of developing prostate cancer, or at least make it more manageable. Research shows that a healthful diet and routine physical activity generally make people healthier and more able to fight disorders and recover from therapies. Specifically, research shows that emphasizing plant sources of food, and limiting the intake of red meat and fats can lower prostate cancer risk. According to the American Cancer Society, tomatoes, pink grapefruit, and watermelon contain antioxidants called lycopenes that help prevent damage to DNA, and by extension may be helpful in lowering prostate cancer risk.

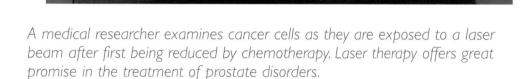

A medical researcher examines cancer cells as they are exposed to a laser beam after first being reduced by chemotherapy. Laser therapy offers great promise in the treatment of prostate disorders.

Despite the debate in the medical community about prostate cancer screening, men should at least consider undergoing screening by the time they reach fifty years old. By discussing the pros and cons of screening with his physicians, a man can make informed decisions about the possibility of having prostate cancer. As has been discussed before, the sooner the cancer is discovered, the better the prognosis for treatment, cure, recovery, and survival.

MICHAEL MILKEN AND THE PROSTATE CANCER FOUNDATION

No celebrity has done more to advance prostate cancer research than has Michael Milken. In 1993, after completing a two-year prison sentence for violating securities laws, the junk bond king was diagnosed with advanced prostate cancer and told he had eleven months to live. Stunned by the news, the forty-six-year-old former financial executive, who had a great

Michael Milken (left) poses with Nomar Garciaparra at Fenway Park prior to a Boston Red Sox home game in June 2004 to promote the Prostate Cancer Foundation's Home Run Challenge. Each June, Major League Baseball allows fans to make pledges for each home run hit in sixty major league games designated as Home Run Challenge games. The fundraising drive raised more than $2.1 million in 2004.

reputation for supporting medical research, was also surprised by how little he knew about the disease.

Milken was even more surprised to learn that not much was being done about prostate cancer. At the time, few grants were being awarded to fund prostate cancer research, which was then considered a black hole, because of a presumed lack of new ideas. Consequently, medical researchers were reluctant to submit proposals to study the disease. Milken immediately responded to this desperate situation by founding and committing $25 million to CaP CURE, which later became the Prostate Cancer Foundation (PCF).

Today, the Prostate Cancer Foundation is the largest source of charitable support for prostate cancer research in the world. According to its Web site, since its founding in 1993, the PCF has "raised more than $230 million and provided funding for prostate cancer research to more than 1,200 researchers at 100 institutions worldwide." It has been a major force for prostate cancer research over the last decade. Moreover, its grants have led to significant advances in the treatment of the disease, as well as the general understanding of its pathology.

The PCF solicits funding from government sources, corporations, and individuals. It also finances public awareness campaigns.

Medical researchers and the business community point to Michael Milken's advocacy for raising the spotlight on prostate cancer. In a November 1, 2004, *Forbes* magazine article, Robert Langreth writes: "Prostate cancer, once a research backwater, is suddenly sexy thanks to the work of one patient: Michael Milken."

Although there is widespread disagreement among physicians and medical researchers about whom to screen and treat for prostate cancer, modern approaches to prostate cancer have resulted in earlier detection and more effective treatment. Researchers continue to explore new methods of diagnosis and treatment that will, by their effectiveness, win wide acceptance within the scientific community, as well as offer hope to the large percentage of men who are likely to be diagnosed with prostate cancer.

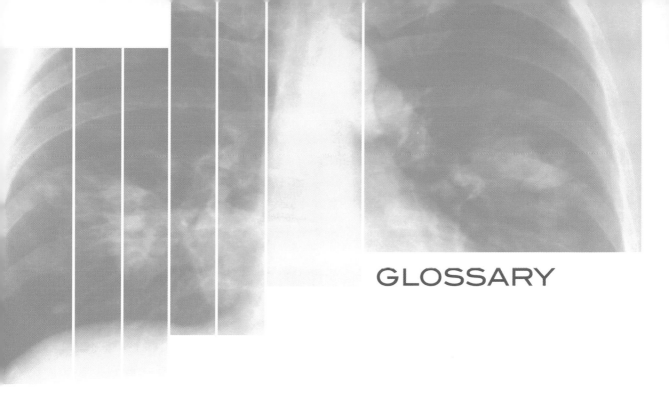

GLOSSARY

adenocarcinoma Cancer arising from glandular cells.

adolescence The period during which a child develops adult characteristics under the influence of sex hormones.

anatomy The structure of an organism.

asymmetry Dissimilarity in different parts of a structure; unbalanced proportions.

benign Not cancerous.

benign prostatic hypertrophy Common condition among older men in which an enlarged prostate impedes urine flow.

biopsy To take a sample; the process of taking a sample.

cancer A medical condition marked by an out-of-control growth and reproduction of abnormal cells.

cell The smallest self-functioning unit in all living things.

chemotherapy Treatment with anticancer drugs.

colonoscopy An examination of the colon with a flexible tube that has a light and a camera on one end.

constrict To cause to narrow; to impede passage.

diagnosis Identification of a medical condition or disease through examination by a physician.

digital rectal exam (DRE) A technique in which a physician inserts a finger into a patient's rectum to feel for abnormalities.

distend To expand.

DNA (deoxyribonucleic acid) The material within the nucleus of a cell that carries genetic information.

ejaculation A reflex during which semen is ejected through the penis during orgasm.

erection A reflex during which the penis fills with blood, stiffening it.

gene A unit of DNA that contains the information for a specific function; the functional unit of heredity.

gland An organ that secretes hormones or produces fluids.

impediment Something that impairs progress or success.

impotence The inability to achieve an erection.

induration Firmness.

lymphatic system A system of vessels connecting lymph nodes; part of the immune system.

lymph node A collection of immune cells.

malignant Cancerous.

metastasis The spread of cancer.

nodularity Quality of having irregular bumps.

obesity The state of being overweight to the point of having health consequences.

pathology The causes, development, and progress of disease, and how it affects the body.

physiology The dynamic function of an organism.

prognosis Chance of recovery.

prostate A gland that produces much of the fluid in semen.

prostate cancer A malignant tumor arising in the prostate.

prostate-specific antigen Protein secreted into the blood by the prostate gland; useful in diagnosis of prostate cancer.

prostatic intraepithelial neoplasia Precursor to prostate cancer.

replication The process by which DNA manufactures a copy of itself.

semen Fluid produced by the prostate gland that carries sperm during ejaculation.

staging The process of determining the extent of a cancer.

suture A technique in which two parts of a tissue are sewn together.

testosterone The male sex hormone.

therapy Treatment.

tumor A mass of excess tissue that results from abnormal cell reproduction.

urethra Tube passing from the bladder, through the prostate, and continuing through the penis; transports urine and semen.

FOR MORE
INFORMATION

American Cancer Society
(800) ACS-2345 (227-2345)
Web site: http://www.cancer.org

American Institute for Cancer Research
1759 R Street NW
Washington, DC 20009
(800) 843-8114
Web site: http://www.aicr.org

National Cancer Institute
(800) 4-CANCER (422-6237)
Web site: http://www.cancer.gov

Prostate Cancer Foundation
1250 Fourth Street
Santa Monica, CA 90401
(800) 757-CURE (757-2873)
Web site: http://www.prostatecancerfoundation.org

Prostate Cancer Research Institute
5777 West Century Boulevard, Suite 800
Los Angeles, CA 90045
(310) 743-2110
Web site: http://www.prostate-cancer.org

WEB SITES

Due to the changing nature of Internet links, the Rosen Publishing Group, Inc., has developed an online list of Web sites related to the subject of this book. This site is updated regularly. Please use this link to access the list:

http://www.rosenlinks.com/cms/prca

FOR FURTHER READING

Clifford, Christine. *Our Family Has Cancer, Too!* Duluth, MN: Pfeifer-Hamilton Publishing, 1997.

Fromer, Margo Joan. *Surviving Childhood Cancer: A Guide for Families.* Oakland, CA: American Psychiatric Press, 1995.

Harpham, Wendy Schlessel. *Becky and the Worry Cup: A Children's Book About a Parent's Cancer.* New York, NY: HarperCollins, 1997.

Marks, Sheldon, M.D. *Prostate and Cancer: A Family Guide to Diagnosis, Treatment, and Survival.* 3rd ed. Cambridge, MA: Perseus Publishing, 2003.

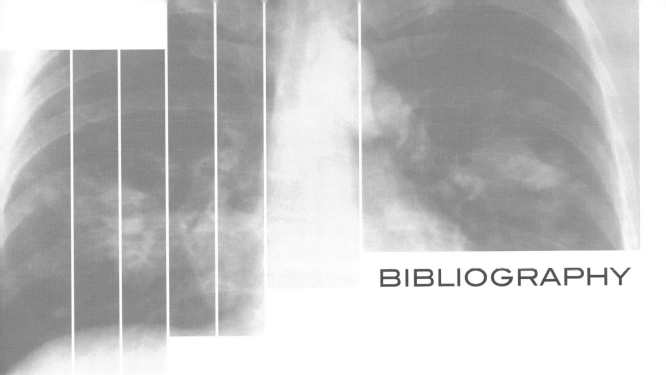

BIBLIOGRAPHY

Humphreys, M. R., et al. "Minimally Invasive Radical Prostatectomy." *Mayo Clinic Proceedings*, September 2004, Vol. 79, No. 9, pp. 1169–1180.

Kaufman, D. S., et al. "Case 21-2004: A 63-Year-Old Man with Metastatic Prostate Carcinoma Refractory to Hormone Therapy." *New England Journal of Medicine*, July 8, 2004, Vol. 351, No. 2, pp. 171–178.

Korman, H. J. "Prostate Cancer: Radical Perineal Prostatectomy." Emedicine.com. Retrieved September 2004 (http://www.emedicine.com/med/topic3053.htm).

Miles, B. J. "Open Prostatectomy." Emedicine.com. Retrieved September 2004 (http://www.emedicine.com/med/topic3041.htm).

Naitoh, J., et al. "Diagnosis and Treatment of Prostate Cancer." *American Family Physician*, December 1998, Vol. 57, No. 7, pp. 1531–1539.

Nelson, W. G. "Prostate Cancer." *New England Journal of Medicine*, 2003, Vol. 349, pp: 366–381.

Oesterling, J. E. "Benign Prostatic Hyperplasia: Medical and Minimally Invasive Treatment Options." *New England Journal of Medicine*, 1995, Vol. 332, pp. 99–109.

Theodorescu, D. "Prostate Cancer: Brachytherapy." Emedicine.com. Retrieved September 2004 (http://www.emedicine.com/med/topic3147.htm).

Theodorescu, D. "Prostate Cancer: Management of Localized Disease." Emedicine.com. Retrieved September 2004 (http://www.emedicine.com/med/topic3186.htm).

INDEX

ABOUT THE AUTHOR
Dr. Mark Stokes practices medicine in the North Shore Long Island Jewish Health System in New York, one of the nation's largest health systems. A graduate of SUNY-Stony Brook School of Medicine, he specializes in internal medicine. As a primary care doctor, he helps coordinate the diagnosis and care of cancer patients. He is also a lecturer and an associate program director for graduate medical education in the Department of Medicine at North Shore University Hospital.

PHOTO CREDITS

Designer: Evelyn Horovicz; Editor: Wayne Anderson
Photo Researcher: Hillary Arnold